W9-CDD-431

CAPTAIN PAJAMAS

BRUCE WHATLEY

ROSIE SMITH

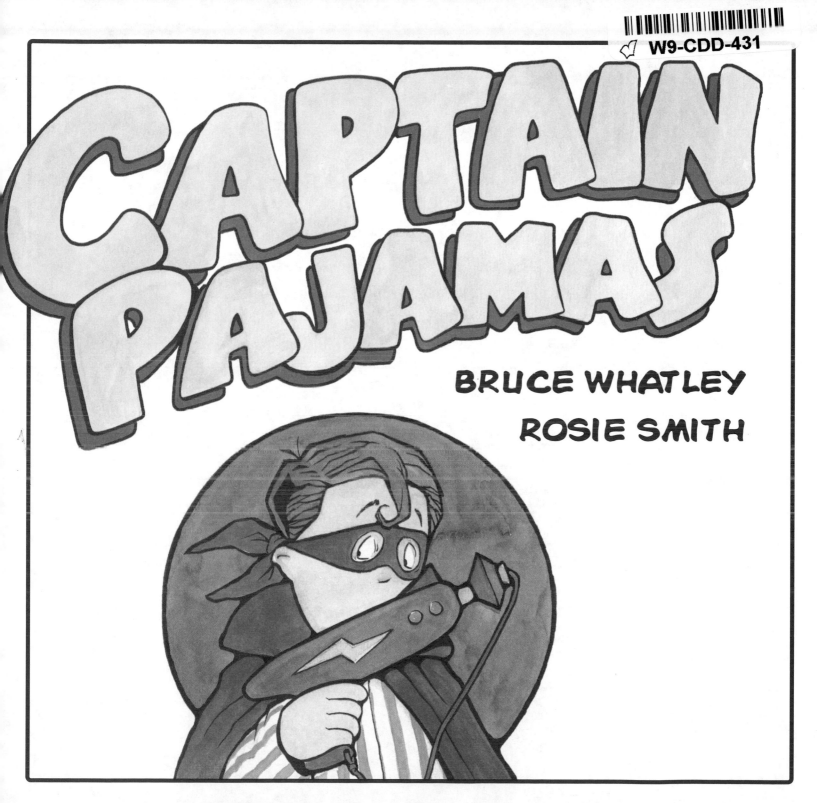

HARPERCOLLINSPUBLISHERS

For Matt, Melissa, Rich, and Kay.
Many thanks.
Bruce & Rosie

Captain Pajamas
Text copyright © 2000 by Bruce Whatley and Rosie Smith
Illustrations copyright © 2000 by Bruce Whatley
Printed in the U.S.A. All rights reserved.
http://www.harperchildrens.com

Library of Congress Cataloging-in-Publication Data
Whatley, Bruce.
  Captain Pajamas / Bruce Whatley, Rosie Smith ; [illustrated by Bruce Whatley].
    p.   cm.
  Summary: In the middle of the night, Brian transforms himself into Captain Pajamas,
Defender of the Universe, to save his older sister Jessie from attacking aliens, but they
are nowhere to be found.
    ISBN 0-06-026613-9. — ISBN 0-06-026614-7 (lib. bdg.)
    [1. Heroes—Fiction.   2. Extraterrestrial beings—Fiction.   3. Imagination—Fiction.]
I. Smith, Rosie, 1954–   II. Title.
PZ7.W5485 Ca 1999   98-3211
[E]—dc21   CIP
                                                                           AC

Reprinted by arrangement with HarperCollins Publishers.
10 9 8 7 6 5 4 3 2 1
❖

It was the middle of the night.
Mom and Dad were asleep.
My sister, Jessie, was asleep.
I was awake.

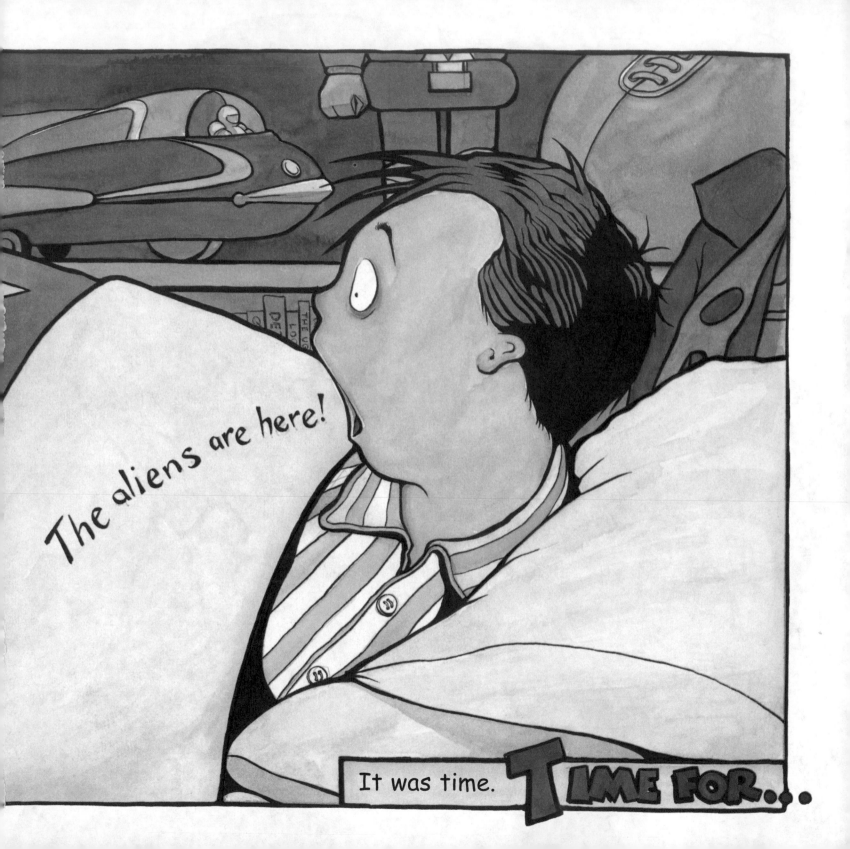

And his trusty dog, **SHADOW.**

I strapped on my utility belt and crept into my sister's room.

In my Captain Pajama's super voice, I said . . .

We sneaked down the hall and peeked around the corner.

WHIRRR... PLONK!

WHIRRR...PLONK!
WHIRRR...PLONK!

So much for your aliens, Brian!

There _are_ aliens, and they are here because the light on my alien communicator came on!

I led Jessie to my Pajama Cave. There, on the floor, was the Captain Pajama Remote-Control, Techno-Robotic Alien Communicator.

Shadow looked cleaner than he had ever looked before.

I don't think Jessie cared about Shadow being clean.

To the untrained eye Shadow may have looked a little guilty.

I tiptoed into
the living room.
Jessie got the light.

Jessie didn't agree.

NOW GO TO BED, BRIAN!

I thought about zapping her with my Remote Control, Alien Detecting, Hydro-Self-Aiming Laser Gun. But then I remembered. I was

CAPTAIN PAJAMAS

Defender of the Universe. I had to hold myself to higher standards.